THE FAMILY BOOK

TODD PARR

Megan Tingley Books

LITTLE, BROWN AND COMPANY
NEW YORK BOSTON

Little, Brown and Company

Hachette Book Group
1290 Avenue of the Americas, New York, NY 10104
Visit us at LBYR.com

Little, Brown and Company is a division of Hachette Book Group, Inc.
The Little, Brown name and logo are trademarks of Hachette Book Group, Inc.

First Paperback Edition: May 2010
Originally published in hardcover in October 2003 by Little, Brown and Company

Library of Congress Cataloging-in-Publication Data

Parr, Todd.
  The family book / by Todd Parr. — 1st ed.
  p. cm.
  "Megan Tingley Books"
  Summary: Represents a variety of families, some big and some small, some with only one parent and some with two moms or dads, some quiet and some noisy, but all alike in some ways and special no matter what.
  ISBN 978-0-316-07040-9 (pb) / ISBN 978-0-316-73896-5 (hc)
  [1. Family—Fiction. 2. Individuality—Fiction.] I. Title
PZ7.P2447 Fam 2003
[E]—dc21   2002036843

20 19 18

IM

Printed in China

To my family—who sometimes
did not understand me,
but encouraged me to
go after everything I wanted
even when we did not agree.
As I now realize—this takes
a lot of love to do.

—T.P.

Some families are big.

Some families are small.

Some families are the same color.

Some families are different colors.

All families Like to HUG each Other!

Some families live near each other.

Some families live far from
each other.

Some families look alike.

Some families look like their pets.

All families are Sad when they lose Someone they Love.

Some families have a stepmom or stepdad and stepsisters or stepbrothers.

Some families adopt children.

Some families have two
moms or two dads.

Some families have one parent instead of two.

All families like to celebrate special days together!

Some families eat the same things.

Some families eat different things.

Some families like to be quiet.

Some families like to be clean.

Some families like to be messy.

Some families live in a house by themselves.

Some families share a house with other families.

All families
each other

can help
be STRONG!

There are lots of different ways to be a family. Your family is special no matter what kind it is.

♡ Love, Todd